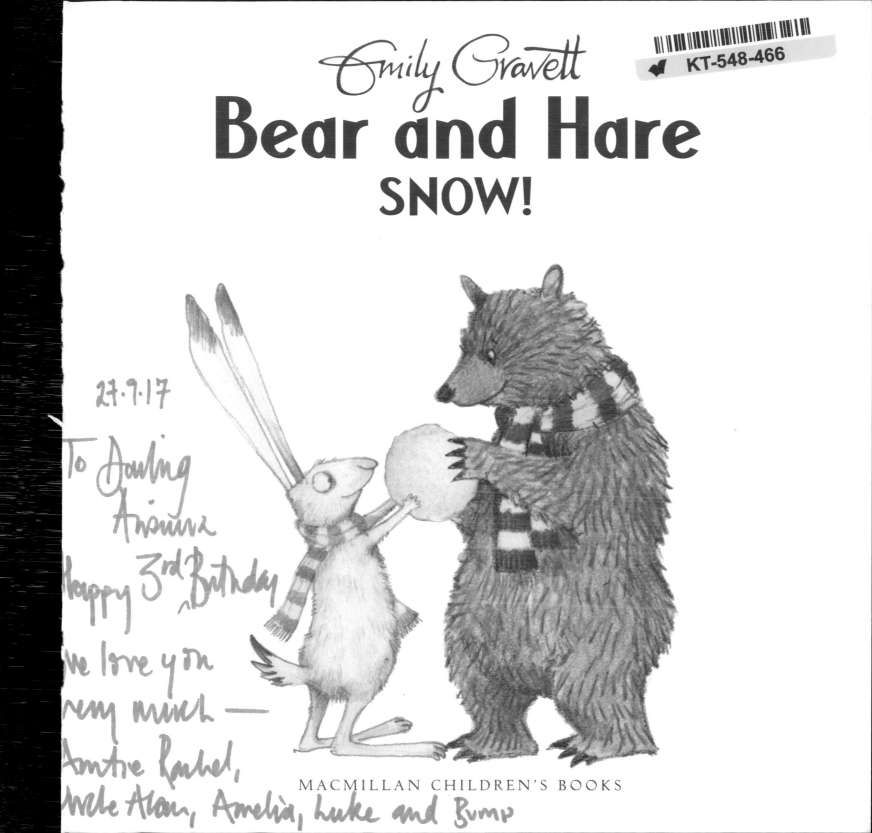

Emily Gravett

Bear and Hare
SNOW!

27.9.17

To darling
Arianna

Happy 3rd ~Birthday

we love you

very much —

Auntie Rachel,

Uncle Alan, Amelia, Luke and Bump

MACMILLAN CHILDREN'S BOOKS

One morning, Bear and Hare
went outside and saw . . .

OW!

Hare loves snow.

Bear and Hare caught snowflakes
on their tongues.

They made snow prints,

and snow angels.

Snow hares,

and snow bears.

Bear rolled a big snowball,

and Hare rolled a little snowball.

LOTS of little snowballs!

Then Bear and Hare went . . .

Home?

SLEDGING!

Hare and Bear LOVE snow!

First
published 2014 by Macmillan Children's Books

a division of Macmillan Publishers Limited

20 New Wharf Road, London
N1 9RR
Basingstoke and Oxford
Associated companies throughout
the world
www.panmacmillan.com
ISBN: 978-1-4472-7323-3

Text and illustrations copyright © Emily Gravett 2014
Moral rights asserted.

1 3 5 7 9 8 6 4 2

A CIP catalogue record
for this book is
available from
the British
Library.
Printed
in
China

For Fin